I LIKE TO BE LITTLE

by Ann Matthews
illustrated by Eleanor Mill

A Golden Book · New York
Western Publishing Company, Inc.
Racine, Wisconsin 53404

I like to be little, because, being little, I can do very special things.

I'm just the right size to smell all the pretty flowers.

Only little people can ride on rocking horses.

Because I'm little, my daddy and
I both fit in the big chair while he
reads to me.

I get to play with toys in the bathtub. I give my dolly a shampoo, or I play games with my tiny tugboat and sailboat.

Sometimes I splash and kick and
pretend that I'm a ferocious alli-
gator in a pond!

I can even run under the table
without bumping my head.

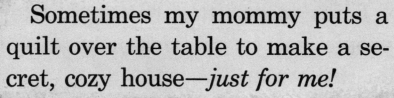

Sometimes my mommy puts a quilt over the table to make a secret, cozy house—*just for me!*

I like to be little, because little people get to go trick-or-treating on Halloween.

It's fun to dress up in a scary costume, too. *Boo!*

Big people pick me up and lift me high in the air and say, "Upsy-daisy!" Sometimes my head almost touches the ceiling!

I like to sit in my mommy's lap
and have her rock me.
She sings pretty songs to me.

Because I'm little, I can play in a cardboard box. Yesterday the box was a fire engine.

Today the box is a boat!

A big friend pulls me in my new red birthday wagon.

Or I can ride in the bumper seat
of my daddy's bicycle.

I like to be little, because my dog
and I are just about the same size.

Mommy rakes our yard. It's fun
to ride in the wheelbarrow with all
the dry, crackly leaves.

I fit just right in the seat of a grocery cart.

I help my daddy pick out good things to eat.

I can go around making up silly
poems—just because I'm little.

Playing with things in the kitchen is fun! I build tall towers and big buildings with cans and boxes.

I make lots of music by beating on pots and pans.

Most of all, I like to be little because my mommy and daddy always tuck me into bed and give me good-night hugs.

Being little is special!